Words to Know Before You Read

cozy
crunched
eagerly
huddled
peered
rummaged
shelter
snuggled
stooped
twitched

www.rourkeeducationalmedia.com

Edited by Precious McKenzie
Illustrated by Ed Myer
Art Direction and Page Layout by Renee Brady

Library of Congress PCN Data

In the Doghouse / Kyla Steinkraus
ISBN 978-1-61810-199-0 (hard cover) (alk. paper)
ISBN 978-1-61810-332-1 (soft cover)
Library of Congress Control Number: 2012936800

Rourke Educational Media
Printed in the United States of America,
North Mankato, Minnesota

rourkeeducationalmedia.com

customerservice@rourkeeducationalmedia.com • PO Box 643328 Vero Beach, Florida 32964

In the Doghouse

By Kyla Steinkraus

Illustrated by Ed Myer

Jonathan sat on the couch and stared out the window. Two feet of snow had fallen the night before. It was a snow day! Yay!

In his backyard, snow covered the ground like a soft, white blanket. Icicles hung from the trees. The sky was cold and gray.

Jonathan's golden retriever snuggled against him. "Aren't you glad we're warm and cozy inside, Gizmo?" Jonathan asked as he stroked Gizmo's fur.

Suddenly, Jonathan saw
something move inside the
doghouse in the backyard.

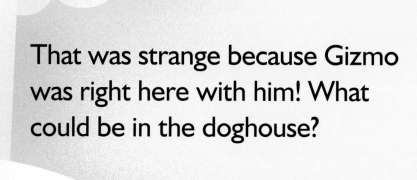

That was strange because Gizmo was right here with him! What could be in the doghouse?

Jonathan crunched through the snow
to the doghouse.

He stooped down and peered into the doghouse.
It was dark but dry inside.

A small, white rabbit huddled against the back of the doghouse. Her nose twitched.

Jonathan raced back inside the house. "Mom!" he cried. "There's a rabbit in the doghouse!"

"What do you think she's doing there?" Mom asked. Jonathan thought about it. "She probably wanted to get out of the snowstorm."

Mom nodded. "I think you're right."
"Could she stay in the doghouse for a little while?"
Jonathan asked.

"I don't think Gizmo will mind," Mom said. Gizmo wagged his tail. Gizmo liked being in the warm, snug house.

15

"I bet it's hard to find food in the winter," Jonathan said. "Could we give her something to eat?"

Jonathan and Mom rummaged through the refrigerator until they found some delicious fruits and vegetables. Perfect rabbit food!

Jonathan placed apple peels, carrot tops, and spinach leaves outside the doghouse door.

After a while, Jonathan went back outside to check on the rabbit. Not only was the food gone, but now there were three rabbits inside the doghouse!

19

Jonathan went outside to check on the rabbits after dinner. The rabbits had multiplied! There were so many rabbits, they could hardly fit inside! They all twitched their noses at him.

"Mom! We need more food," Jonathan yelled.

After several days, the snow melted. Jonathan checked the doghouse. How many rabbits would there be? But, the rabbits were all gone!

Jonathan was glad all the rabbits had a warm place to rest and a good meal during the cold, snowy days. Gizmo was glad to have his doghouse back!

After Reading Activities

You and the Story...

What did Jonathan find in the doghouse?

Why do you think there were rabbits in the doghouse?

How did Jonathan help the rabbits?

Have you ever helped an animal?

Words You Know Now...

Synonyms are words that have similar meanings. Write one synonym for each word below:

cozy	rummaged
crunched	shelter
eagerly	snuggled
huddled	stooped
peered	twitched

You Could...Feed the Wildlife in Your Own Backyard

- First, talk to your mom and dad to get permission before you put out food for the animals.

- Squirrels and chipmunks like to eat:
    - Cracked corn or cobbed corn
    - Sunflower seeds and peanuts
    - Regular bird feed
    - Small table scraps

- Rabbits like to eat:
    - Greens, parsley, and carrot tops
    - Green beans, peas, and apple slices
    - An occasional carrot for a treat

About the Author

Kyla Steinkraus lives in Tampa, Florida with her husband and two children. Luckily, none of the animals in her backyard have to worry about winter. In Florida, it is nice and warm all year!

Ask The Author!
www.rem4students.com

About the Illustrator

Ed Myer is a Manchester-born illustrator now living in London. After growing up in an artistic household, Ed studied ceramics at university but always continued drawing pictures. As well as illustration, Ed likes traveling, playing computer games, and walking little Ted (his Jack Russell).